CONTENTS

The White Cat   7

Naughty Sophie   33

Master Wind and Madame Rain   57

The Bluebird   83

Gilda and the White Lake   109

The Four Little Girls   133

Adapted from stories by
Madame d'Aulnoy, the Countess
of Segur, Paul de Musset,
Monique Gorde
Translated from the French and re-told by
Maureen Spurgeon

Illustrations Copyright © by Lito Publishers
English text Copyright © by Brown Watson (Leicester) Ltd
Published in Great Britain by Brown Watson (Leicester) Ltd.,
55a London Road, Leicester LE2 0PE
All rights reserved throughout the world
ISBN 0 7097 0486 0
Printed in Czechoslovakia
50265/3

MY OWN

Fairyland

TALES

Brown Watson

ENGLAND

The White Cat

Once upon a time, there lived in a huge castle an old king who had three sons, each one as brave and as handsome as the other.

Now, the king was beginning to feel tired, because he had reigned for many years. So he decided to give up his throne to one of his sons.

But the three young princes were all so kind and so brave that their father did not know which one to choose.

After a lot of thought, he called all three together and told them:

"My sons, I am now too old to reign for much longer, so I have decided to give up my throne to one of you. And the son who can bring me, in a year, the smallest dog in the world, will be the next king!"

"I shall go to the south!" said the eldest. "I have high hopes of finding what I want there!"

"I shall go to the east!" said the second. "And I hope, dear father to bring you what you desire!"

"As for me," said the youngest, "I think I shall go to the north. And perhaps I shall be lucky in my search. . ."

So the three princes embraced their father, as he wished them good fortune. Then each one went on their way.

The youngest prince, as he said, went towards the north. Set astride his young, white horse, he rode through towns and villages, searching everywhere for a dog small enough to please his father.

But all the dogs he came across seemed so very big, and, somehow he had to carry on with his search.

"Still, if I find what I want, it will all be well worthwhile!" he thought, not wanting to be defeated for a moment.

Then, one day, as he rode out of a village, he found himself at the edge of a vast forest, so dark and so thick that it seemed quite impossible to go any further.

"I shall have to go back the way I came!" the prince thought, rather gloomily. "It's useless to search for a dog hereabouts! But first, we shall have a drink, my horse and I!"

A cool stream trickled along near the forest border, so he let his horse drink a little first, then dismounted to help himself to some of the fresh, clear water.

He was just about to go on his way, when he saw an old woman coming towards him carrying a pitcher-jug.

"Handsome prince!" she cried. "Would you be so kind as to fill my pitcher with water?"

"Yes, of course!" the good prince smiled.

The old woman came a little closer.

"I know what you are looking for!" she whispered. "Despite what you think, you must go deeper into this forest! There, all your wishes will come true, believe me! Even more than you ever hoped for!"

The prince decided to take the old woman's advice. Very soon, he was going deeper into the forest, riding all day long without even seeing another living soul.

By nightfall, he was wondering if it had all been a joke. Then, suddenly, a storm broke out, the wind whistling and making everything whirl fiercely around him.

Lightning flashed – and the prince saw a path leading up to a big castle at the top of a hill.

With a glad cry, the prince spurred his horse on, and soon came to the most beautiful white castle he had ever seen.

He got down from his horse and banged on the door, crying out:

"Hello! Is there anyone there? I am lost and I need shelter for the night! Can you let us into your castle, just me and my horse?"

No sooner had he finished speaking, than the door opened wide before his eyes. Nobody appeared – but, to his great surprise, the prince could see at either side of the door hands which seemed to appear from nowhere, each one carrying an enormous candelabra.

Then, other hands appeared, making the prince even more astonished. Some were waving him on, signalling for him to follow, whilst others led his horse to the stables.

With those hands as his guide, the young prince was led into a great, big room with the loveliest of furniture, and a fire burning brightly in the hearth.

Soaked through to the skin because of the storm and the rain, the prince went to warm himself. Then the hands took off his wet clothes and brought him a splendid suit of velvet and a shirt made of silk. And at last, when he was dressed, the hands led him into another huge, brightly-lit room. . .

That was when the prince saw a sight which made him open his eyes wider still. Because, at the top of the stairs, sitting on a pile of lace-trimmed cushions, there sat the most delightful, adorable little cat with shining white fur.

She had a crown on her head, and her huge golden eyes looked at the prince so sweetly and with such kindness that he was completely enchanted, and bowed low.

"I am delighted to meet you!" he said, most respectfully. "Tell me, does all this belong to you?"

With a gracious bow of her dear little head, the white cat nodded to the prince, and said to him in such a soft, gentle voice:

"Welcome to my castle, where I am very happy to receive you! Will you do me the honour of joining me for dinner, this evening?"

"With great pleasure!" answered the prince – as the long ride in the driving rain and howling wind had made him feel very tired. But now, with dry clothes and the promise of a good meal, it seemed he hardly remembered it at all.

"Then come this way, if you please!" said the cat.

And she led the prince into yet another large room, in the middle of which was a most beautiful table, laden with all sorts of delicious foods.

The cat and the prince sat facing each other, whilst the mysterious hands served them with everything needed to make the perfect meal.

And, as they ate together, they began talking, as friends

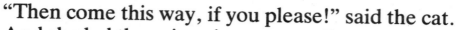

do, of one thing and another. The prince was both amazed and charmed to discover how very clever and wise the white cat was. Altogether, it was a most pleasant evening.

All too soon, it was time to go to bed, and the prince went to his room feeling very happy. But, in the corridor, he noticed the portrait of a young man so much like himself that he gasped in surprise.

"Who can that possibly be?" he wondered aloud.

But he was so tired that he could not think any more about this new mystery. Instead, he slid down inside his bed, gave a delighted stretch, and was soon fast asleep.

Next day, the moment he opened his eyes, he knew that he really did not want to leave the beautiful castle.

"How I'd love to stay here," he said to himself, "especially with that lovely little white cat!"

And with a long, sad sigh, he went to say goodbye to her. But, the cat said:

"I would be very happy if you could stay a little longer!"

The prince was too pleased to argue. So, he stayed with the white cat, becoming happier with each day that passed.

He soon learned that only cats lived at the castle. The white cat gave parties and dances, and there were quite a few concerts where all the musicians were cats as well.

Time passed, and the young prince loved being with the white cat more and more. She was always so sweet and so gentle, as well as being very clever. Also, she seemed to like the prince being there, and, whenever he spoke of leaving, she would talk him into staying just a little longer. . .

Days, then months passed, with the prince and the white cat talking together, going for walks in the castle grounds, holding parties and doing all sorts of interesting things.

Then one evening, to his horror, the prince realised that he had been at the castle for a whole year. And he was supposed to be bringing his father the smallest dog in the world by the next day!

"What can I do?" he said to the white cat, very worried. "Not only have I not found the smallest dog in the world, but it is a three day journey to reach my father's palace!"

"No need to worry!" comforted the white cat. "I shall lend you my magic horse – and in a few minutes you will be at your father's side. Then open this walnut before the king's eyes – and inside there will be what he has asked for!"

So, with many thanks, the prince took the walnut, and leapt on to the magic horse – a horse carved most beautifully from wood, but which galloped at such speed that in no time at all the prince found himself at the old king's palace.

The two other sons were already there. Both had brought a tiny, tiny dog – the first was even smaller than an orange, but the other was hardly as big as a tangerine!

"So!" they said to their brother. "Show us what you have brought!"

There was a hush, as the young prince took the walnut from his pocket. Under the somewhat stern gaze of the king, he cracked it open – and there to everyone's great surprise, appeared. . . the smallest dog in the whole, wide world!

"You have certainly won this test, my son!" declared the king. "But – I do not have to give up my throne at once. . . In fact, I think I shall reign for just one more year!"

"Just as you please, father," said the young prince.

"And this time," the king went on, "I shall give my throne to the son who will bring me a length of cloth so fine, that it can pass through the eye of a darning needle! Go, then – and the best of good fortune to each of you!"

"I shall go to the west!" said the eldest, "and I will not stop searching until I find what you ask!"

"Then I shall go to the east!" cried the second son. "Such fine cloths can often be found in Japan and China!"

"As for me," murmured the youngest with a secret smile, "I shall go to the north once more. . ."

And he at once began thinking of his sweet friend, the white cat, hardly able to wait until he could see her again. As soon as his two brothers had said their farewells, he leapt into the saddle of the magic wooden horse, which had been waiting patiently for him.

The horse at once galloped away, faster than the wind. In the twinkling of an eye, it had sped through the forest where the prince had been lost, coming to a halt in front of the beautiful white castle.

The prince jumped down, went inside, and found himself in the

room where, sad and all alone, the white cat sat on a heap of cushions.

"Here I am, my dear friend!" cried the prince joyfully. "See, I have come back to you!"

"Oh, my prince, how happy I am to see you again!" mewed the pretty cat. "I have been so sad whilst you were away!"

The prince was soon telling her all that had happened at the king's palace.

"So, I returned at once to you," he finished off, "so that I could spend another year with you!"

And, once again, the prince became completely enchanted. One happy day followed another so quickly that all too soon another year had passed.

"The time has come for you to return to your father," the cat reminded him, looking sad once more. "Go then, my prince – and please take this with you. . ."

So saying, she gave the prince a hazelnut. Then, with a last, tender hug for his dear friend, he leapt on to the magic wooden horse, who, with his amazing speed, arrived in just a few minutes at the old king's palace, where everyone was already waiting.

The two others had brought cloths of great beauty, so wonderfully fine that each one easily passed through the eye of a darning needle.

But when it came to the youngest prince – why, he broke open the hazelnut, and took out a length of cloth so fine and so delicate that the very finest cloth seemed thick beside it.

And, with no trouble at all, the prince threaded it through the eye of a darning needle – not once, but many, many times, and then, even through the eye of an ordinary sewing needle, too!

"You have certainly beaten your brothers, once again," the king told his youngest son. "And, yet – I think I shall reign for another year. Then I shall step aside, and hand over my throne to the prince who will bring me the fairest and sweetest of sweethearts!"

So, once again, the three princes set off – the youngest astride the magic wooden horse, riding like the wind to be at his friend's side once more. And how happy they were to see each other again, with the cat rubbing herself against the prince, as he tenderly stroked her white fur.

"So, have you returned for another year, my dear prince?" she purred.

The prince told her what the old king had decided – and the year passed, more wonderful than ever before.

"It is time for you to return to your father, my sweet prince," the cat said miserably, "with a beautiful sweetheart to present to him!"

The prince sighed, then shook his head.

"This time," he whispered, "I shall not return. I could never leave you again, for I know I shall never be happier with any sweetheart

than I have been with you!"

"My prince," the cat answered lovingly, "I know a way of pleasing your father, and granting both your happiness and mine. . ."

"How is that?" the prince asked at once.

"I shall tell you. . ." the white cat took a deep breath. "No matter how you dread it, you must kill me!"

"Kill you?" cried the prince in horror. "Never, my sweet, white cat – never, could I do such a dreadful thing!"

"But, I tell you that by killing me you will bring us both so much happiness. . ."

"I do not want to hear anything more!" shouted the prince. "I would never have any happiness if you were killed! Why, I should be broken-hearted, you know I would!"

Again and again, the white cat kept asking, but the young prince always refused to do what she wanted.

Then, one night, the prince had a strange dream. He saw in his sleep the old woman whose pitcher he had filled two years ago.

"You must obey your friend, the white cat," she told him. "She has her reasons for wanting you to act this way. Tomorrow, you must do as she asks – and do not be afraid!"

The young man woke up at once with a troubled mind. He went to talk to the white cat, finding her very sad.

"If you do not kill me," she told him, "I shall have to spend my whole life like this. I beg you, my dear prince, not to be afraid – and to kill me!"

So, at last, the prince, closing his eyes tight so as not to see the dreadful deed which he had to do, brought down his sword on to the beautiful white furry head. . .

And, at that very moment, an extraordinary thing happened! The cat vanished completely – and in her place, a beautiful young girl stood smiling into the eyes of the astounded prince.

"H-how could this happen?" he stammered in amazement.

And at that same moment, throughout the castle, all the cats became handsome gentlemen and beautiful ladies, all coming forward to greet the lovely young girl.

"Princess!" they cried, bowing and curtseying low. "At last, we are freed from the evil spell cast upon us!"

Seeing how astounded the prince looked, the young girl began to tell him her story.

"Once," she said, "some wicked witches sent this terrible dragon into my father's kingdom, killing and destroying everything in its path. My father did not know what to do, so the witches said to him:

"If you want us to take the dragon away from your kingdom, then you must give us your only child, the princess!"

My father was very sad – but he had to agree in order to save his people. So, they took me away, and made me their servant.

Then, when I was fifteen years old, a young lord saw me and fell in love with me. He wanted to marry me, but the witches made the dragon kill him. Then they locked me up with everyone whom I loved in a lonely castle, in a forest so deep and so thick that nobody could ride through it. . ."

"Then," the princess went on, "they gave us servants, the magic hands, and, in the end, we were all changed into cats."

"You will never get back your human form," they cackled at us, "until a young man exactly like the one our dragon killed is brave enough to come into the forest, enter the castle, then fall in love with a dear little white cat, and agree to kill her!"

"Then, just as we were beginning to lose hope," smiled the young princess, "because we could see no end to our sad state – why, you came along, my sweet prince, and saved us all!"

"And how happy I am!" cried the prince, full of joy. "I cannot wait to take you back to my father's palace and present you to him. Then, we shall marry – if you will have me. . ."

"Yes. . ." murmured the princess. "Oh, yes. . ."

Very soon, they were both riding on the magic horse which took them through valleys and forests, going faster than ever before.

"Faster!" cried the prince, hardly able to wait. "Faster!"

As for the princess, her two arms were around her sweetheart as she pressed herself against him, her head spinning with the speed of the ride until the king's palace came into sight, and the wooden horse came to a halt, the prince and his princess dismounting together.

The young prince took his sweetheart by the hand, and they went into the palace.

The two other princes were already there – and each of them had brought a beautiful young maiden to present to the king.

One by one, each of the princes came before the king, and said:

"My father, may I present to you the girl I wish to marry. She is kind and good, and I know that you will like her!"

The old king looked closely at the three princesses, not knowing which to choose. They were all so beautiful. He stroked his white beard thoughtfully, looking quite uncomfortable at not being able to choose.

At that moment, a huge siamese cat came into the room and began rubbing itself against the king's legs, purring all the while.

The first princess turned up her nose in disgust.

"I cannot bear cats!" she declared. "Just being in the same room as one makes me feel quite ill!"

The second burst into tears.

"I hate cats!" she sobbed. "They tear into everything with their horrid claws! I beg you, please keep it away from me, before it pulls at my lovely dress!"

As for the third princess – she remembered that, not so long ago, she herself had been a cat. So she knelt down and took the animal in her arms, stroking it gently, and saying with a smile:

"Me? I just love cats! They are always so clever, so gentle and affectionate!"

Now, it so happened that this siamese cat was the favourite pet of the old king, and seeing it rubbing its nose against the princess and purring so loudly, His Majesty knew the choice which he had to make.

"You shall succeed me as king!" he told his youngest son. "As from tomorrow, I shall step aside, and we shall celebrate your wedding!"

And so it was done. The young prince became king, and, to the delight of everyone, married the one he loved.

The prince and princess were so happy, and had three children called Timmy , Tabby and Tibby.

"Mummy," said her youngest daughter one day, "why do we all have cats' names?"

"Because," said the queen with a sweet smile, "your Daddy fell in love with a little white cat!"

Naughty Sophie!

Strong, full of mischief and never short of energy – that was four-year-old Sophie Ryan, who lived with her Mummy and Daddy in a house in the country.

Nearby lived Camille and Madeleine, two little girls who often came to play with Sophie in her lovely, big garden which spread out all around her house. Her cousin, a boy called Paul, usually joined them in the school holidays, and they would spend many happy days together, with Sophie's Mummy looking after them all.

SOPHIE'S WET HAIR

Sophie's Mummy always said that she really needed two pairs of eyes to look after her daughter, because, although Paul, Camille and Madeleine were always good and did everything they were told, Sophie was inclined to be naughty and greedy, and not at all obedient.

One afternoon, when the others had gone into town, Sophie was reading by herself. Soon, she began feeling bored. And – after teasing the canary by shaking the poor bird's cage – she sat down in front of her dressing table mirror, tugging at her thick, black hair.

"It's not fair!" she burst out. "Why can't I have long, blonde hair, all curly, like Camille? People are always saying how nice it is! Those ringlets of hers, they're always so pretty when they're tied with ribbons to match her dress!"

And with a long, gusty sigh, she sat scowling at her rather untidy-looking hair, tied up in two bunches like sheaves of shaggy corn, either side of a chubby, pink face with a turned up nose – and a rather thin, discontented mouth. . .

Just then, she heard the wind beginning to rise up, with bursts of raindrops lashing the windows of her room. Now. . . she thought, Camille was always complaining that the least bit of dampness made her hair curl up so much that she could hardly get a comb through it. . .

"So. . ." Sophie, said to herself, "if my hair was soaked in the rain, it would be just as curly as Camille's! What a lovely surprise that would be for Mummy and Daddy! But – I had better do it all in secret, otherwise they are bound to start telling me off, as usual. . ."

Very quietly, she opened the door and looked up and down the corridor. The coast seemed to be clear! Her own nursemaid was busy working on the other side of the house, and so was nowhere to be seen! So, naughty Sophie opened the window and stuck her head right

outside, into the driving rain. Trouble was, the wind had changed direction, so all Sophie got was a fine sort of drizzle. . .

"I'll get nowhere like this!" Sophie grumbled, very annoyed.

And it was then that she noticed quite a shower of water pouring down from a gutter at the back of the house. . .

"Perfect!" she pronounced. "I'll get what I want in no time, standing underneath that! By the time I'm finished, there'll be no more of these silly, black bunches! I'll be curly by tea-time this evening!"

So, that naughty little Sophie, not caring what her Mummy might say, stood right under the gutter pipe – and, to her great delight, got a shower of rainwater over her neck, her arms and her back.

And when she was all wet, she went back inside and wiped her head with a handkerchief, taking great care to flick up her hair.

Suddenly, her mother came in! She was absolutely amazed and dumbfounded to find Sophie with her hair sticking up all over the place, looking so scared and so wet that she wanted to laugh.

Instead, she said: "You have disobeyed me, as usual, you little madam! So, you can come down to tea just as you are, so that Daddy and Cousin Paul can see what a sight you look! Never mind if you are cold – you can stay here, in your room. The view is very nice, especially if you want to see your friends playing in the garden!"

So, when Paul came back with Sophie's Daddy, both of them stopped in surprise when they saw Sophie, looking so ashamed and so silly in her rain-soaked clothes.

"What's all this about?" her Daddy asked, quite amazed

"Sophie made up her mind to be naughty, and now she looks dreadful!" Mummy said. "For her punishment, she's going to have tea just as she is!"

"Oh, Aunty, can't you forgive her?" Paul pleaded.

"I'll promise, I'll never do it again!" added Sophie.

So, Sophie's Mummy relented, and just made Sophie change her clothes. And, Sophie? She decided that all she wanted to make her hair look pretty were some nice, new ribbons!

THE BLACK CHICK

For a little while, Sophie made up her mind to be such a good girl. But – oh, dear! Once again, she did not do as she was told – and a poor little animal had to suffer because of it. . .

Each morning, Sophie would go to the farmyard with her mother to see which eggs had been hatched, and the new-born chicks.

One day, as she came into the hen-house, she saw a magnificent chick, with feathers as black as jet. But, when Sophie and her Mummy tried to get a little nearer, the hen snapped at the black chick with great big pecks of her sharp beak.

Sophie's Mummy felt sorry for the black chick, and gave it a few drops of water to comfort it a little, saying:

"I do not think we should leave this black chick with the mother hen. . . It would be best if we took it back home with us!"

"Put it in my toy basket, Mummy!" cried Sophie. "I shall take care of it, and when it is better and grown a little bigger, we can put it back in the farmyard!"

"Good idea!" agreed her Mummy. "Take it with you to your room, and keep an eye on it there. Mind you, it will take up a lot of your time, what with cleaning its wounds where the hen pecked it, then feeding it every day, and seeing that it stays in the warm and does not escape. It will be a wonderful chance for a madcap like you to show that you can be caring and unselfish!"

And Sophie was so delighted with her little pet that she did all she was told, caring for it so well that, just one month later, it had grown into such a pretty little chick. But now it was more difficult to watch, because it often went for a stroll in front of the house, scampering away on its little claws and going to scratch about under the hedge. In the end, Sophie's Mother decided to take it back to the farmyard, and explained her reasons to Sophie.

"Besides," she finished up, "you know that foxes often come this way. They could easily catch your black chick and carry him off!"

Sophie couldn't help feeling sad. "When you are bigger," she said to the black chick, "we shall be able to run around the kitchen garden. But, for now – well, just look out for vulture-birds!"

For a little while, Sophie was quite sensible, taking no notice of the sad chirps from her black chick. After being used to the house and kitchen garden, he felt very bored shut up in the farmyard!

Then, bit by bit, Sophie got into the habit of seeing her little pet in secret. She would often take it behind the house, where it would have fun pecking around for gnats and worms in the grass.

At first, Sophie stayed close to the black chick, watching it closely. Then, little by little, she grew careless, playing with her dolls when she should have been looking after the black chick.

Then, one day, Sophie happened to glance up from her toys – and saw a huge bird with a great, pointed beak stepping slowly towards the black chick, watching it, and getting ready to pounce, whilst the poor chick could only stand stiff with fright.

All at once, the bird pounced on the chick with a savage cry, snatching it up in its claw then flying away high into the sky.

Hearing all the noise and the squawks, Sophie's Mummy came out.

"You are a naughty, disobedient girl!" she shouted angrily. "You took the black chick from the farmyard, and now he has gone for ever!"

And Sophie could only weep bitter tears for the lovely little pet she had lost.

THE DONKEY

After losing her black chick, Sophie was good and well-behaved for two whole weeks. So her Mummy wanted to reward her, and brought home a lovely little grey donkey!

"Ooh, isn't he lovely?" cried Paul and Sophie, as the gardener led it into the courtyard.

Sophie's Mummy had also brought a saddle and a stool, so that the children could mount the donkey easily. She told them not to leave the grounds, and never, ever to be cruel to the little animal. So, the very next day, Paul and Sophie decided to try it out, taking it in turns to ride the donkey. Sophie got in the saddle first, and rode off towards a little wood near the very edge of the grounds.

But Sophie soon began complaining that the donkey did not go nearly fast enough for her. Before long, she had cut a rod from a hazel tree, and began to whip the poor animal with all her might. Rather surprised, the donkey turned its huge eyes towards her, twitched its long, silky ears. . . but, do you know, he would not go any faster!

"Don't hit him like that!" cried Paul, most indignant. "You'll hurt him!"

"I want him to get a move on!" shouted Sophie. "You wait till I prick him with a spur!"

"But – we don't have a spur!" Paul almost choked. "That would be cruel!"

But, nothing would stop Sophie. She ran back to the house to find the sewing box, and took out a big darning needle. Then she put the eye of the needle into the heel of her shoe, leaving a good half inch sticking out to give a sharp point.

"You know that your Mummy said we should never be cruel to the donkey!" cried Paul, very angry. "You'll dig into his side with that!"

But Sophie just jumped into the saddle and gave the donkey a kick.

At once, the donkey went off at a gallop, going so fast that Sophie was so frightened that she had to hang on to the reins. In her panic, she dug her heel more firmly into the donkey, who began to kick, and then to jump wildly, throwing Sophie over his back before he finally took flight, the dust from the path flying under his shoes!

Stunned by the fall, Sophie lay flat on the ground, until Paul came to help her up, her nose and her hands bleeding and badly grazed. As for the donkey, he had disappeared – probably gone back to the stable, Paul thought.

The two children could only turn around and go back to the house, where both their mothers were waiting to ask them lots of questions.

"Your donkey came back here at a fine old gallop, seeming very scared!" they said. "We were told he was so gentle and good-natured, and yet he rushes back home without either of you riding him. And what a state you are in, Sophie! What happened?"

"Oh," said Sophie, trying to look as if it didn't really matter, "it was nothing, Mummy, nothing at all! The donkey suddenly began to kick, and then he threw me to the ground. That's how I grazed my nose and my hands, but I'm quite all right!"

Sophie's Mummy glared fiercely at Paul, who turned away, very red in the face. Then she looked again at Sophie, watching her carefully from head to toe.

"Why are you walking like that, Sophie?" she asked. "Have you bruised your ankle, or something? Show me at once!"

And that was how Sophie's Mummy discovered the needle in her shoe, the "spur" Sophie had made. Only it was hurting Sophie this time. Now she knew what had made the donkey bolt, and she was very angry.

"Well!" she burst out. "For being so cruel, you can stay in for a whole week without riding your donkey, you naughty girl!"

Poor Sophie! Her holidays were spoilt – and it was all her own fault!

CREAM AND HOT BREAD

Sophie's Mummy knew that eating too much was no good to anyone, and she always said as much to her daughter – whom she knew would never resist food, especially when it came to eating between meals. As for Sophie, she just said she had a big appetite, and ate almost everything she could lay hands on.

One day, Lucy the maid said to Sophie: "Cream and fresh bread for supper tonight, Sophie!"

And, leaving Sophie alone in the kitchen, Lucy went off to do something else.

Now, the bowl of cream was within easy reach, together with the sweet-smelling bread. So it was not long before Sophie had cut herself a thick slice of fresh bread, and spread the cream on top.

And when Lucy came back a little later, there was Sophie at the table, gobbling greedily away. Lucy was very angry.

"How could you have eaten all that?" she gasped. "You will make yourself sick! What will you say to your Mummy if she finds you ill – to say nothing of most of tonight's supper having gone?"

"Oh, do calm down, Lucy!" sighed Sophie. "I was feeling hungry – so, how can I possibly be ill? This cream is very nice, you know, and we still have some fresh bread for supper, hot from the oven!"

And, taking her mid-morning snack, she went out to play with her doll. But, not long afterwards, she began to feel very sorry for herself. The cream and hot bread lay heavily on her stomach, and she had a headache, too. She sat in her little chair, and stayed there quite still, her eyes closed.

Surprised at the sudden silence, her Mummy came out at once and found Sophie looking pale and rather ill.

"What is wrong, dear?" she asked, hurrying across and seeming quite worried. "Have you eaten anything to make you ill? Please, tell me!"

Sophie hesitated, then answered in a whisper: "No, Mummy. Nothing at all!"

But Sophie's Mummy knew her rather well. . .

"I think you are telling me fibs! So I am going to see Lucy, and I know that she will tell me the truth!"

And with that, Sophie's Mummy went back into the house, leaving Sophie looking as pale and as pasty-looking as the doll which she held on her lap.

When she came back, she was very angry. She put a hand on Sophie's burning forehead and took her to her room, calling out angrily for Lucy.

With Lucy helping her, Sophie's Mummy undressed her and put her into bed, Sophie feeling much too unhappy to say anything. And all the time, her Mummy was scolding poor Lucy, saying that she ought to have known that Sophie was too greedy to be left alone in the kitchen.

Then she turned to Sophie.

"You've been up to your tricks again, you little madam!" she cried, sitting beside Sophie's bed. "Lucy told me that the farmer's wife left the cream and fresh bread in the kitchen, and you gobbled it up while her back was turned! How often have I told you not to eat between meals?"

"And now," Sophie's Mummy went on, "it's the worst for you! Beause you will not be able to go to tea tomorrow at your cousin Paul's, along with Camille and Madeleine. So, instead of playing games in the woods and picking flowers and wild strawberries, you'll have to stay here by yourself, all alone in your room, with only some broth for supper!"

Sophie, who was already feeling sick enough, could think of nothing to say, and turned her head away, beginning to cry into her pillow, and wishing she could say she was sorry to Lucy.

She spent a very bad night, suffering with headache and stomach pains. But the next day was even worse, not being able to go and see Paul, missing the tea party and all the fun in the country. Twice, she spilt medicine on her pillow, and, for being such a greedy little girl, could only have sour drinks, nasty-tasting medicines and thin soups. . .

For two long days, she felt ill and had to stay in bed. The very thought of cream and hot bread made her think she would never be able to eat them again.

After that, she sometimes went with Paul and her friends Camille and Madeleine to the farms in nearby villages. Everyone around her enjoyed eating the warm bread and cream – all except Sophie. . . The sight of that thick cream and crusty bread made her remember how ill she had been, and she began feeling sick again.

And if anyone offered some to her, she always refused, most politely. Of course, everybody said how sensible and well-mannered she was.

Only Sophie knew that her dislike of fresh cream and warm bread was the price she had paid for being greedy.

THE WOLVES

One day, Sophie's Mummy called Paul and Sophie.

"I am going to the farm, taking the dogs for a walk through the forest," she said. "You can come too, on condition that you stay close to me, so that you do not get lost!"

The two children were very excited, looking all around as they went along. On the way, they passed Camille and Madeleine's house, and asked if they would like to come, as well. And at first, the children walked quietly just behind Sophie's mother.

But Sophie soon noticed some wild strawberries growing along a grassy slope, and stopped at once.

"Keep close to me, Paul!" she whispered. "Look, let's pick some strawberries and have a little feast! I've brought a basket!"

"No," replied Paul very firmly, "I do not want to disobey my aunt and run the risk of getting lost in the forest!"

"Then, do what you like, you coward!" Sophie stormed. "Me, I want to start eating, right now!"

"I am no coward," Paul told her. "You get lost in the woods if you want to, but I'll do what Aunty says, and nothing else!"

And so Paul hurried off to catch up with Sophie's Mummy, as she walked briskly along with the two other little girls and the dogs.

Suddenly – she noticed two fierce, bright eyes, moving along through the undergrowth. Then there was the sound of twigs cracking as huge, furry paws drew nearer. . .

Sophie's Mummy went very pale and called out to make sure all the children were with her. But, of course, naughty little Sophie did not answer. . .

"Where's Sophie?" she gasped in fright.

"She stayed behind to pick strawberries!" Paul explained, going rather red in the face.

"Oh, no!" shrieked Sophie's mother. "And we are being followed by wolves! We must go back quickly and get her!"

And she dashed off, back along the forest path, followed by the two girls, Paul and the dogs.

They reached Sophie just as the two wolves, with their jaws open and claws outstretched, had come out of the undergrowth and were getting ready to pounce on Sophie – who, by this time, could only stand absolutely petrified with fear.

Armed with a stick he had picked up along the way, Paul threw it in front of the wolves, making the dogs chase after it, barking furiously as they surrounded the beasts. After what seemed like ages, the wolves were seen off, back to where they had come from – but not before one of the dogs had been bitten. . .

And all this time, Sophie stood quite still in the middle of the path, her overturned basket at her feet and trembling with fear.

"Have you no sense, Sophie" sighed her mother at last, when all danger had passed. "Look, you were only saved because of Paul, but one of our dogs was badly bitten, and you have spoilt the whole day for all of us!"

And Sophie, still very pale and frightened, put her arm around her Mummy's neck, then hugged Paul.

"Oh, Mummy! I'm so very sorry. And, as for you, Paul – how could I possibly have called you a coward?"

Paul just smiled, and took the injured dog in his arms, and they went home.

Feeling very sorry for what she had done, Sophie took great care of the poor animal, and, a few weeks later, it was well enough to caper around in the park – much to the comfort of the stupid, little girl.

But she never forgot what had happened in the forest, and, at the very mention of wolves, she would go quite pale and begin trembling from head to foot.

It was then that she made up her mind to become as good and as clever as her cousin and her friends, Madeleine and Camille. But – that was such a difficult thing for her to do! No matter how hard she tried to keep out of mischief, it seemed she just could not help getting into trouble again!

Still, Sophie's Mummy did see that her daughter was really trying to be good, and decided to give her a nice treat.

So, on a beautiful summer's afternoon, she invited all the village children to join Paul, Madeleine and Camille in a party for Sophie.

And, what a lovely day it was!

The table was set out in the dining room, with all sorts of delicious things to eat. The children wore their very best clothes and everyone was so pleased to see Sophie eating politely and looking after her little guests as well.

The animals were not forgotten, either. Grey Tabby-Cat lapped her milk, whilst the dogs who had so bravely protected the children gnawed at their bones.

Then there were sing-songs, and dancing, games and Blind-Man's-Buff in the garden. . . And all through the day, Sophie did not do one single naughty thing.

But what she remembered most was the start of the meal, when Paul had given her a lovely present and said:

"Well done, Sophie! You have become a most charming cousin, and I am indeed proud of you!"

Master Wind and Madame Rain

There was once a miller called John-Peter, who had a little cottage, a small vegetable garden – and an old windmill.

Trouble was, the wind hardly ever blew strongly enough to turn the sails of his mill, so he could never grind enough wheat to make flour. And, as the rain never seemed to fall on his garden, his vegetables did not grow, either.

John-Peter was very unhappy about it.

"Ah, Master Wind!" he cried out one day. "If you could only blow on my windmill! And you, Madame Rain, if you could just have the goodness to water my vegetable garden, you would do me such a great service!"

But, it was all in vain.

Now, John-Peter, feeling rather lonely in his windmill, took for his wife a pretty country girl called Claudine, and she began to rear hens and rabbits which John-Peter would sell at the market of a nearby town.

So, for some time, the miller and his wife were happy. And soon, they had a son called Robert.

Then, suddenly – disaster struck the little house. Claudine became very ill, the hens and the rabbits died one after the other, and the day came when there was just no money left at all.

One evening, John-Peter could stand it no longer.

"Master Wind!" he cried. "Madame Rain! Please, please help me!"

Hardly had the words been spoken, when John-Peter heard a loud rumbling.

"W-what is happening?" he gasped, very frightened.

At that moment, the cottage door burst open in a gust of wind – and a most extraordinary figure came into the room. The man was so big that his head bumped against the ceiling, so vast and so huge that he seemed just like an enormous balloon. Two beautiful wings quivered on his back, yet he seemed as light as air, his feet hardly seeming to touch the ground.

"Who are you?" gulped John-Peter, politely offering the most comfortable chair in the cottage.

"I am Master Wind! Did you not call me? Well, here I am! So, tell me – what is it you want?"

John-Peter found it quite easy to share his worries with Master Wind, who then thought for a little while.

"Good miller," he said at last, "since you have welcomed me so kindly, I shall come sometimes with my breezes, my gales, and my good storms to turn the sails of your windmill. If ever you need me, just come and see me in my secret dwelling-place. I live in a cave, high up on the hill. You cannot mistake it – the entrance is covered by an enormous heap of leaves, and the branches of the poplar trees are all quite bare. Now, I must go and organise a storm in the Pacific Ocean, and I have a long way to go. Goodbye, then – and good luck, my miller friend!"

And Master Wind left so swiftly that he was gone before John-Peter knew it.

As soon as he had gone, another person made an appearance in the little cottage. And she was even stranger than Master Wind. Her eyes were full of tears, she was sneezing without stopping, there were raindrops under her veil, and she wore a scarf the colour of a rainbow around her shoulders.

In fact, she was so wet that the miller led her to the fireplace to dry herself. She refused, quite horrified.

"Why," she said, "I am Madame Rain! I heard you asking for me just now! I see that you are a wise man, and I do like your kind welcome – so I promise to come to you when you need me. At the dawn I shall send my dew, and in the evening, my rain-fall will water your garden. If you ever need me, come to see me in my cave by the sea, and I shall help you. Now, I must go and start crying over London! Good-bye!"

And Madame Rain went the way she had come.

61

Master Wind and Madame Rain kept their word, and, what with one blowing and the other raining, the sails of the windmill began turning in rhythm, the kitchen garden was filled with magnificent vegetables, and the miller started feeling more peaceful and free from worry. Then Claudine gradually got better, and Robert became the most popular and the cleverest boy for miles around.

Sadly, the miller's wife was a chatterbox. Her husband had not said one word about the two visitors he had had. Not a whisper about the promises of Master Wind, nor about the good services of Madame Rain. And nothing at all about the hill, nor the cave beside the sea. John-Peter took great care to keep his secret!

But, near at hand, there lived a cruel and a greedy lord – and everything he saw, he wanted. . .

And one morning, as the lord went riding near the miller's land, he noticed how the sails of the windmill turned so easily, and the vegetables in the garden growing with such strength and life, with John-Peter humming to himself as he worked.

"There's been a miracle here!" thought the lord jealously. "What a lovely windmill! And those beans are even better than the ones I've grown! Why should they be so much better here, in a humble cottage garden than in fine castle grounds? Why, this miller makes me look a fool! I'll have to make him pay for this, so that I may share in his new-found fortune!"

"Hey!" he roared, riding his horse at a gallop up to John-Peter. "I'll have ten pieces of gold for tax tomorrow, or I shall thrash you!"

And the jealous lord continued on his way, taking no notice of poor John-Peter's cries of protest.

Next morning, when the miller had paid out the ten pieces of gold which the lord had demanded, he only had a little bit of money left in his pocket.

Seeing this, Claudine began to cry.

"Oh, all the misery is starting again!" she wept. "What will become of us?"

"Now, do not fret yourself, Claudine!" urged her husband. "I shall try and sort this out!"

And without saying any more, he wrapped himself up in his old cloak and went to the top of the mountain, where a dreadful storm was already breaking out. He went straight into the cave of Master Wind, and told him about the cruel lord, and all that had happened.

"Calm yourself, miller!" whined Master Wind. "I shall help you, never fear!"

And he brought a wand, along with a dear little barrel carved in silver.

"Take these two gifts," said Master Wind, "and any time you need help, give one tap of the wand on the side of the barrel, and you shall see what you shall see!"

John-Peter gratefully took the presents from Master Wind, thanked him, and went back home.

And when John-Peter put the wand and the silver barrel on the little table, Claudine just stood and stared. Never had she seen anything quite so beautiful.

"Oh, do tell me where these came from!" she cried. "Let me into your secret, please do!"

So, the miller told his wife about his wonderful adventures, making her promise not to tell anyone, just in case the cruel and jealous lord ever got to hear about it.

Then, when it was supper-time, he tapped the pretty barrel with the wand, hoping for a good feast.

At once, the barrel opened out, like a curtain, to reveal a charming little kitchen, with lots of tiny little cooks, all running to their places.

Next, there were lots of tiny little servants to lay the table with a tea-set just big enough for a doll. Then they all went back inside the barrel and it closed up after them.

Then, everything – dishes, plates, bottles, food – they all became normal size. And as the miller and his family were very hungry, the marvellous meal was quickly eaten all up, before they went to bed dreaming of the magic wand and the silver barrel.

If only that chatterbox Claudine could have kept the secret to herself! But she was soon telling her next-door neighbour about the barrel. The next-door neighbour told the milkmaid – and she hurried across to tell the cook who worked at the lord's castle. And he repeated it to the castle steward – so that, by that very same evening, the greedy lord had learned of John-Peter's good fortune!

"This wonderful barrel would be of more use at my castle than at the miller's cottage!" he thought, going quite green with envy.

So, early next day, he mounted his horse and galloped off to the mill, offering John-Peter a fine bag of gold to buy the little barrel. He talked for a long, long time, saying how the miller could buy lots of splendid things for his home and the finest of food with a purse bulging with gold coins. . . and in the end, John-Peter was so tired of listening to him that he agreed to accept the offer.

The greedy lord snatched up the magic barrel at once – but without giving John-Peter the promised bag of gold. . .

Soon afterwards, Claudine bcame ill once again. So John-Peter had no choice but to go to the top of the hill and tell Master Wind how foolish he had been to trust the wicked lord.

But, almost as soon as he had begun to explain what had happened, Master Wind flew into a stormy temper.

"Idiot!" he bellowed. "You stupid miller, you deserve to be taught a lesson!"

John-Peter looked so unhappy and so scared at these words that Master Wind cooled down almost at once, and gave him another wand with a barrel made of gold. Then he shut the door without saying anything more.

John-Peter could hardly wait to get back to the mill and tap the golden barrel with the wand. But – oh dear! There was only a puff of smoke. . . which became a huge giant, which thrashed the miller!

Then, the giant faded away into a puff of smoke once more, and shrank back inside the barrel.

Very hurt and upset at all this, John-Peter stayed in bed for ten days – which gave Claudine a little time to think. And she decided that the wicked lord must be taught a lesson for tricking John-Peter with the promise of gold in exchange for the silver barrel.

So, she went around the village telling everyone that the miller now had a little golden barrel!

Of course, the greedy lord soon heard the news, and rode at once to the mill. Seeing the golden barrel, he was so struck by its shining beauty that he offered to buy it there and then.

"Very well!" smiled Claudine. "It's yours for a thousand pieces of gold!"

Pleased at getting such a splendid bargain, the lord sent a servant to fetch the thousand pieces of gold from the castle vaults, and left the windmill quite overjoyed at having got the precious barrel.

The moment he got back to his castle, the wicked lord went down into his dungeon, eager to see what would happen. He took out the wand, tapped the little golden barrel. . . and from the very centre there arose a cloud of fire which formed into the enormous giant. . . and he spanked the greedy lord very soundly indeed!

"This is all that wretched miller's fault!" gasped the wicked lord, almost choking with anger and fury. "I'll make him suffer!"

And after that, hardly a week passed without the lord and his friends going hunting near the windmill and riding their horses across the garden and vegetable plot.

John-Peter tried to protest – but the lord always began planning something even worse for the following week. It was a very hard time for the miller and his family.

At last, the wicked lord charged all the farmers who lived on his land double taxes to pay for wars and battle – and poor John-Peter found he was ruined.

"Oh, dear! Oh, dear!" sobbed Claudine. "Whatever shall we do, now?"

That was when the miller remembered Madame Rain. . . So, wrapping himself in his cloak and scarf, he set out on the long road which led to the seaside.

What a journey! The rain fell down in bucket-loads, a thick mist hid almost everything from sight, and the only sound was the cries of seagulls as they swooped down. But John-Peter pressed on, until, at last he reached the beach and began searching for Madame Rain's cave.

After what seemed like ages, he found it, and called out: "Hello! Madame Rain?"

"What do you want, miller?" she answered, coughing, sneezing and sniffing all at once.

"Oh, Madame Rain!" cried poor John-Peter. "If only you knew what has happened. . ."

And he began to tell Madame Rain of his many misfortunes over the years, talking a little of his young son, Robert, who was not yet seven years old but could already read better than his father.

"Then," said Madame Rain, "if your son is so clever, you must give him this box and magic wand and this gold-edged book. With such brains, he will soon be able to make himself a fortune!"

John-Peter tried to thank Madame Rain, but she was too busy coughing and sneezing into great piles of paper hankies. So he took the gifts and went straight back to his windmill to show his wife all that Madame Rain had given him for their son.

"Oh, no! Not that!" whispered Claudine, who had not forgotten the second, golden casket. "Supposing a great big giant comes out of the box?"

But, when Robert tapped the magic wand on the book and the box, they both opened at once. In one there was the copy of a play, and in the other a little theatre complete with lots of scenery and puppets in lovely costumes.

Robert knew exactly what to do. And as he announced the title of the play, the little stage of the theatre lit up, and the curtains rose. Then he began to read all the parts, and the puppets started to talk and to act just like the real actors.

"Why!" breathed Claudine. "It's beautiful!"

"How clever our child is!" thought John-Peter proudly.

The miller and his wife, who had never had the chance or the money to be able to afford to leave the mill, could hardly believe their eyes. Quite dazzled by the little theatre, they enjoyed the puppet plays every evening, beginning to dream almost before their heads touched the pillow.

But, once again, the jealous and wicked lord heard what had happened. . . .

"So!" he snarled. "John-Peter has a magic theatre! Such luxury would be far better at my castle than at his mill! I shall go at once and fetch it back to amuse my children whilst I am away!"

So the greedy lord went straight to the miller.

"Miller!" he roared. "Give me your toy theatre to keep my children happy whilst I am away fighting in the wars!"

Robert heard this. And he did not trust the wicked lord at all.

"This theatre is mine!" he said. "And I shall never give it away!"

"But," he added, for he did not want the lord to make more trouble for his father, "to please your children, I should be willing to come and show it to them at the castle!"

And, of course, the lord had to accept Robert's kind offer.

For many months afterwards, the young boy often went to the castle with his toy theatre. And, because the lord's wife was generous and kind, she sometimes gave him a piece of gold as payment.

Some time later, Madame Rain passed near to the miller's cottage and went inside to rest. And this gave Robert the chance he had been waiting for. . .

Very quickly, he closed the windows and built up the fire in the hearth. Madame Rain's eyes began to dry up, her cough stopped as if by magic, and her voice cleared. But, far from being pleased, she cried out:

"Oh, no! I have completely dried out! Oh, let me go back to the seaside! I cannot live without my friends, the great waves!"

But Robert took no notice, and shut her up in a cupboard.

Next day, Master Wind was on his way to John-Peter's mill. And, as before, Robert closed all the doors and windows, leaving Master Wind without any air, and making his voice thin and wavering.

"I am choking!" he groaned. "Air! I must have air!"

But, do you know, that naughty Robert shut Master Wind up in the cupboard along with Madame Rain, and cried out to his two prisoners:

"If you follow my orders and do just as I say, then I shall free you!"

Master Wind and Madame Rain each cried out in protest, but Robert would not change his mind.

Very slowly, the grandfather clock ticked the hours away without either side giving in.

But, two days later, with Madame Rain more dry than an autumn leaf and Master Wind as flat as a burst balloon, the talking began.

"Robert," said Madame Rain, "if I stay here much longer, I shall be completely dry!"

"And how can I help you, Robert, if instead of blowing I have not the strength to sigh?" pleaded Master Wind.

But Robert would only answer:

"I shall set you free, just as soon as you promise to obey me!"

Madame Rain began thinking longingly of her nice, damp cave, her faithful friends, the ocean waves, and, most of all, the refreshing sea, where she could bathe and visit the underwater cities.

And Master Wind thought sadly of his cave hidden among the dead leaves, the bare trees, and the clouds which hugged the sky. . .

It did not bear thinking about – and both Master Wind and Madame Rain both well knew that there was a chance they would never see their homes again. So, in the end, they decided to give in.

"Robert," they said wearily, "we promise to obey you for as long as you like. Just tell us what you want to do. . .

Now, Robert, with his toy model theatre, had learned quite a lot about the lord and his castle, and he knew that an important naval battle was due to take place in the North Sea.

He had also become very fond of the lord's sweet and gentle wife, and was very sad when she became worried and unhappy because her husband was taking part in the battle, and he wanted to help her, because he had often watched her as she sat with her children, watching the antics of the lovely little puppets.

Robert knew how pleased and happy the lord's wife would be to hear that her husband was safe and sound. So he opened the cupboard, so that Master Wind and Madame Rain could hear what he wanted them to do. Then they waved their farewells, and Robert ran to the castle.

"No need to worry any more, my lady!" he cried joyfully. "With the help of some friends, I shall destroy the whole of the enemy fleet!"

And, so it was! On the orders of the clever boy, Master Wind and Madame Rain left for the North sea, and, between them, they made sure that every ship in the enemy fleet had to turn back!

All this forced the wicked lord to own up to all he had done to the miller – and, from that day onwards, they were never troubled again.

The Bluebird

There once lived in a far land a rich and powerful king, with his queen and their daughter, Flora – a princess so sweet and so pretty that everyone loved her.

Sadly, the queen died, and the king married again. His new wife had a daughter as hard-hearted and as ugly as herself – so ugly, that everyone called her Fish-Face, because her skin seemed to be covered in dry, flaky scales, almost like a fish!

Right from the start, Fish-Face and her mother were both jealous of Flora and her beauty. They treated her so badly, but the kind girl never once complained to her father, the king.

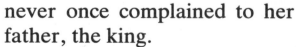

Fish-Face had pretty clothes and went to all the lovely parties held nearby. But poor Flora was dressed in ragged, old clothes – and whenever there was a ball, a banquet or a party, her stepmother would keep her locked up all alone in her room.

Then, one day, a letter arrived at the palace to say that the king of a neighbouring kingdom was pleased to announce the visit of his son, the Prince Charming. The letter also said that if one of the princesses appealed to him, he was ready to marry her.

The palace was at once full of excitement. All sorts of celebrations were planned, the queen being quite certain that the young prince would make an ideal husband for her Fish-Face.

She began ordering lots of beautiful clothes for her daughter, hoping to catch the prince's eye. Flora, of course, would stay in her room throughout the whole of the prince's visit. . .

Well, Prince Charming arrived, and lots of parties were given in his honour. He had to dance with Fish-Face, who always tried in vain to charm him. But, in the end, tired of her being there, he asked the king:

"Haven't you another daughter, Your Majesty? I seem to remember my father speaking of two princesses in this kingdom!"

"But Flora does not like dances nor parties," the queen broke in at once. "She likes being alone in her room!"

"But," insisted the prince, "can I not see her, if only for a moment? I should so much like to meet her before I go!"

"Very well, my friend!" nodded the king. And he turned to the servants.

"Go and fetch Princess Flora from her room!" he commanded. "Tell her that the Prince Charming would like to meet her!"

And, much to the fury of the queen and Fish-Face, Flora soon appeared, pink and smiling. In her plain linen gown she was so pretty that the prince at once fell in love with her.

He did not leave her side all evening, dancing and chatting to her and completely ignoring Fish-Face, who could only sit in a corner, becoming more angry and more jealous every minute.

"Mother!" she said at last to the queen. "Can't you do something?"

"Do not worry, precious," the queen said. "Before the evening is over, I shall go into action!"

Knowing nothing of all this, the Prince Charming and Flora stayed close together, whilst the king watched happily. And as the hours slipped by, the prince knew that he would never love anyone else as he loved Flora.

In the end, he said to her:

"Will you marry me? If you will, then tomorrow I shall ask the king, your father, for your hand!"

Very happy, Flora agreed to become the prince's wife – with the delighted prince promising to make her happy for ever after.

But the wicked queen was furious. Hardly had the ball finished, and Flora back in her room, when she called all the palace guards together. On her orders, they marched the princess away to the heart of a great big forest, where they locked her up in a high, tall tower, cut off from the rest of the world.

Poor Flora was so miserable.

"My Prince Charming!" she cried out in despair. "How will he ever find me here?"

Hardly knowing what she was doing, she went to the one window of her prison, and cried without stopping.

All this time, Prince Charming was very worried about not seeing his sweetheart. He questioned the queen, who always said, with such a cruel smile:

"As I've said, Flora likes to stay in her room. The poor girl is so shy, and hates going out. She likes nothing better than being alone!"

The prince was most disturbed at this, and began to suspect that something was wrong. Flora had seemed so happy at the ball. . . and had she not said that she would marry him? How was it possible that she had disappeared into thin air the very next day? The prince said nothing, but made up his mind to find out the truth.

Next morning, the prince questioned one of the guards, not knowing that he was under orders from the queen. And this guard said to the prince:

"Flora never goes out of her room."

"Then how can I see her?" the prince demanded. "I must speak to her!"

"If it will help you," replied the guard, "I shall tell you a secret. Each evening, when everyone is asleep, Flora goes for a walk in the forest. . ."

The prince made up his mind at once. That evening, instead of going to bed, he would wait for his sweetheart in the forest. . .

He could hardly wait for the day to end, barely managing to be polite to the queen and Fish-Face.

But at last, nightfall came. The prince went up to his room, waiting for everybody to go to bed. And when the moon was high in the sky, he slipped out silently from the castle and went to the forest.

For a long, long time, he waited among the trees, trying to peer through the darkness. He began to get worried, thinking that the guard might not have told him the truth. . . and that was when the shadow of a girl appeared. . .

So happy, he hurried towards her.

"At last!" he whispered. "My sweetheart, I have found you! And how I have missed you!"

He thought he was talking to Flora – when, in fact, it was Fish-Face, hidden beneath a huge cape. . .

Not knowing anything of this trickery, the prince tenderly took the hand of Fish-Face, and slipped a ring on her finger.

"My sweet Flora," he murmured, "let me give you this ring, as a token of our love!"

Fish-Face bowed her head, thinking it best to say nothing. Taking this as a sign of happiness, the prince went on:

"I want to marry you, sweet Flora, because I love you dearly. I can see only too well that your step-mother and sister want to come between us, but they do not matter. It is you, and you alone that I want for my wife. Tell me, is that what you want, too?"

"Yes. . ." Fish-Face answered in a quiet voice, feeling very pleased with herself.

"Then, do not worry. I shall find a way of freeing you from their clutches, and work out a plan so that we may be together for always. Can you meet me here tomorrow night, so that we can talk again?"

"I should like that very much," murmured Fish-Face, taking great care to keep her voice soft and sweet.

"Until tomorrow, then, my sweetheart," whispered the prince. "I shall not fail you!"

And with a joyful heart, the prince went back to his room, hoping to be able to marry Flora before very long.

As for Fish-Face – she went back to her mother in a blaze of triumph.

"My dear mother!" she cried. "Your plan worked perfectly! The prince mistook me for Flora, and I am going to see him again tomorrow night, at the same place!"

"Splendid!" pronounced the queen with a cruel smile. "Now we must go and find a way of celebrating the marriage before he sees through our little plot! Then, once you are his wife, he can do absolutely nothing!"

"How wonderful!" exclaimed Fish-Face, clapping her hands in delight. "I shall be the wife of such a handsome prince! Me – and not that hateful Flora!"

"We must seek the help of your god-mother, the Witch Sarabos!" the queen went on. "Her magic spells will help us, I'm sure!"

(The Witch Sarabos was a wicked witch, with whom Fish-Face had spent many years of her childhood.)

"Tomorrow," the queen continued, "you shall ask the Prince Charming to go with you to your godmother. . . Once there, you can explain everything to her, and she will arrange the marriage!"

"But. . ." faltered Fish-Face, "suppose he sees that I am not Flora? He will refuse to marry me!"

"Do not worry! If that happens, your godmother will put him under a spell!"

Much comforted, Fish-Face went to bed, hardly able to wait for the next day to arrive.

All this time, in her prison high up in the tower, Flora was so unhappy.

"My handsome prince. . ." she sighed, "where are you? How can I find you? Oh, how unhappy I am!"

And she stayed by the one window, spending every day simply looking out into the forest in the hope of seeing her sweetheart prince on his white horse. But, nobody ever came by, and all Flora could do was to cry until there were no more tears to be shed.

The following night, before the chimes of midnight had sounded, Fish-Face went out into the forest wearing an enormous cloak with a hood to hide her face. The prince was already waiting, and, seeing her, he darted forward and took her hands.

"My dear Flora, you are here!" he cried. "I could not wait to see you again! But, tell me – when can I marry you?"

Taking great care to play her part as well as she could, Fish-Face answered softly:

"We cannot marry here, because the queen will try to stop our wedding. So, we must go to my godmother, Sarabos, and get married at her home!"

The prince went wild with joy.

"Trust me, sweet Flora!" he said. "Tomorrow at midnight, I shall come and take you to your godmother!"

Fish-Face hurried away from the prince, pleased to see that he had not recognised her and that her mother's plan was working. . .

As for Prince Charming, he was so eager to marry his sweetheart that he went to find one of his friends who was a magician and told him all that was planned.

"I shall lend you my carriage," said the magician, "then you and Flora will get to her godmother's house that much quicker!"

The prince thanked him – and, at midnight, he met Fish-Face once more in the forest. She had taken care to wear a veil over her face – so, thinking that he was again speaking to Flora, the prince said:

"Come, my sweetheart! We can leave at this very moment, because a carriage is already waiting!"

In they went together, and a pair of winged frogs lifted the carriage high into the air. This way, the carriage could cross miles in an instant, and so soon arrived at the witches mansion.

What a sight that mansion was! It sparkled with the glow of a thousand lights, and its walls were made of crystal and diamonds!

The prince was taken into one room, whilst Fish-Face stayed outside to explain everything to her godmother, putting her arms around Sarabos and lifting the veil to kiss her.

"My dear godmother!" she burst out. "You've simply got to help me! Listen..."

Now, Fish-Face was not very clever, and she had fogotten about the crystal walls. . . She had lifted the veil without thinking, and the prince, in the next room, had seen everything! Knowing then how he had been tricked, he went to escape, feeling both angry and upset. But, at that same moment, the door opened and the Witch Sarabos appeared.

"Prince Charming!" she cackled. "We are going to celebrate your marriage with my god-daughter at once!"

"Never!" cried the prince. "Never! Fish-Face tricked me into this, and I refuse to marry her!"

"But, you promised to marry her!" replied the witch sternly. "You must keep that promise!"

"I promised, because I thought that she was Flora!" retorted the prince. "She alone will be my wife – and no other!"

"We shall see about that!" screeched the wicked witch, working herself up into a fine rage.

And she locked up the poor prince in a dark dungeon underneath the palace.

"You will never come out," she screamed, "until you change your mind!"

Day after day, the wicked witch would come and ask the prince if he would agree to marry her god-daughter, hoping that he would change his mind. But the prince was determined to stay true to Flora. Whatever the Witch Sarabos tried to do, he knew that he could never take the horrible Fish-Face for his wife, not when he was always thinking of Flora.

Three whole months went by. Then, one mornng, the Witch Sarabos finally lost her temper.

"I've had enough!" she shouted. "I am not going to wait for ever!"

And, in a great fury, she tapped the Prince Charming with her wand, crying out:

"You shall become a bird and stay that way until the day you agree to marry my god-daughter!"

No sooner had she spoken than the prince was changed into a magnificent bluebird which at once flew out of the roof-top window which had been left open.

"Now I am free!" he thought with delight. "At last, I can go and find my Flora!"

He flew towards the royal palace, looking all around as he went, 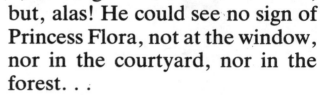 but, alas! He could see no sign of Princess Flora, not at the window, nor in the courtyard, nor in the forest. . .

Refusing to give up, he went on searching fields, villages and woods. . . but Flora was nowhere to be found. . .

Then, when he had searched all over, he caught sight of a deep, thick forest.

As fast as he could go, he flew down towards it, looking for any sign of life. . .

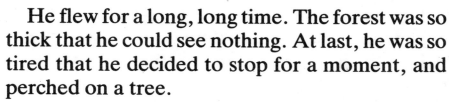

He flew for a long, long time. The forest was so thick that he could see nothing. At last, he was so tired that he decided to stop for a moment, and perched on a tree.

Suddenly, he heard someone weeping. He listened hard, heart beating. Yes – there certainly was crying, then a sweet voice wailed:

"My poor Prince Charming, when will you set me free?"

All of a quiver, the bird flew on towards the voice. Very soon, he saw a high tower, with just one window. And, at the window, he saw – Flora. . .

With a beat of his wings, he perched beside the poor girl and said tenderly:

"At last, my dear Flora, I have found you! I have been looking for you for so long! I am your sweetheart, and I have been turned into a bird by the Witch Sarabos!"

At once Flora knew that it was the voice of her prince. And, in answer to all her questions, the prince told her of the trickery of Fish-Face, the punishment of Sarabos, and all that he had suffered.

"But," he ended, "the important thing is that we are together, now!"

And they were so happy to have each other that they made a promise never to be parted again.

The bluebird built his nest in a nearby tree – and then, every morning, he would perch near Flora, much to her delight. They would stay together each day, chatting, making plans, and hoping for better days to come. He would never leave until the evening, when the jailer would come to close the window and bring Flora her only meal of the day. By night, the prince and Flora slept peacefully, knowing that they would see each other again the next day.

Flora was always so happy after that – and the jailer never heard her cry again. . . He thought this was so strange that he went straight to the palace the moment he turned the key in the lock, and asked to speak to the wicked queen.

"Princess Flora puzzles me these days. . ." he explained. "Until now, she spent all her time weeping. But now, after a couple of days, I hear nothing but laughing and talking – and yet, she is always alone! I do not understand it!"

The queen thanked the jailer for his information. And, when he had gone, she began to think.

"I must find out what is making Flora so happy!" she said to herself. "There is some mystery behind all this!"

She called Fish-Face to tell her what the jailer had said.

"We must look into this!" she declared. "I shall never rest until I find out what has happened!"

"Yes. . ." answered Fish-Face, always very slow to think, "but, what can we do?"

"Well," said the queen firmly, "I shall soon think of something!" And the very next day, she told Fish-Face:

"This evening, we shall go up there to see exactly what happens, close at hand!"

So, when evening came, they went to the tower where Flora was locked up. With the help of the jailer, they both hid in a little cubbyhole, separated from Flora's room by a thick curtain. And it was here that they spent the night in some discomfort.

At last, morning came. They heard Flora getting up, then dressing herself and singing all the time. Hidden behind the curtain, they could see nothing, and quickly grew very impatient.

"Quick!" the queen hissed to Fish-Face. "Get behind me!" And she drew back the curtain most carefully.

Then they both saw Flora running to the window and opening it. All at once, a bird with the most magnificent blue feathers appeared and came to perch on her shoulder.

"My wonderful prince!" murmured Flora, stroking the soft feathers. "How happy I am!"

"Me, too, my sweet Flora!" answered the prince. "Ever since I found you, each day is a joy!"

The queen and Fish-Face were quite dumbfounded with fury as they watched the scene. But, having learned what they needed to know, they backed away into the cubby-hole without a sound.

The two of them quickly returned to the palace, each one seething with rage to know that Flora and her prince were together again.

"We must do something!" Fish-Face kept saying. "We must get them apart, then punish the prince for making me look such a fool and spoiling our plans!"

"Do not worry, my dear daughter," said the queen. "We shall get our own back! Nobody laughs at me and gets away with it!"

"What are you going to do?"

"I shall cast a spell which will put an end to the prince, once and for all!" snarled the queen with a wicked smile.

"Perfect!" crowed Fish-Face. "Serves him right for wanting Flora instead of me!"

The queen lost no time in getting together lots of guards and commanded:

"Take up your bows and arrows! Then you will all go in the direction I shall tell you! And then, if you should see a bluebird, do not falter or hesitate – kill it!"

So the servants, armed wtih their bows and arrows, gathered together in the bushes near the tall tower. Here they waited – and, when they saw the bluebird, they let fly with their arrows to score a direct hit.

Badly injured, the bird fell among the bushes, crying out in a faint-sounding voice:

"Help! Please. . . please help your Poor Prince Charming. . ."

And, standing at her window, Flora heard the dying voice of her sweetheart. But, of course, locked up in the high tower, she could do nothing to help the one she loved. . .

She tried to think desperately how she could help him – but the poor bird had already lost a good deal of blood and was becoming weaker with each moment that passed.

It was then that the princess saw a magic coach pulled by two flying frogs gliding above the forest and coming towards her window!

And in this coach she could see a magician – the same one who had already helped the prince! Worried at not having had news of his friend, he had come to see what was wrong!

"Perhaps this is someone who can help me!" thought Flora, her hopes beginning to rise.

She began to wave towards the coach, crying out:

"Over here! Come this way! My sweetheart, the Prince Charming has been cruelly hurt. I beg you, please come and help him!"

The magician heard her, and ordered his frogs to stop the coach. Then as he stepped down, a faint, weak voice pleaded:

"Please – help! Help me, or I shall die!"

The magician made his way through the trees towards the voice, until he had found the most beautiful bluebird lying on the ground and losing a lot of blood.

The first thing the magician did was to work a spell to make himself invisible, so that none of the queen's guards could see him. Then he took from his cloak pocket a little bottle filled with some special mixture and put a few drops down the bird's beak. Almost at once, the bluebird began flapping its wings, and then opened its eyes.

"Th-thank you my friend," he said, still very weak. "I am the Prince Charming turned into a bird by a wicked witch! Listen. . ."

And the blue bird told the magician all that had happened, from the day when he had borrowed his frog-drawn coach.

When he had finished, the magician, very angry at all that he had heard, cried:

"Do not worry, my friend! I have power enough to destroy the evil spell which the Witch Sarabos has cast upon you! And first, I shall change you back into a human being once more!"

The magician muttered some magic chants known only to himself, and, in just a few seconds, the bluebird became the handsome prince that he was before.

"And, now, Prince Charming," said the magician, "we are going to free your sweetheart!"

So they went back to the high tower, where the magician chanted yet another magic spell. Then the prince raced up the winding staircase, bounding the steps two at a time. Like a tornado, he burst into Flora's room, where she sat at the window looking very unhappy.

"Flora!" the prince cried out. "Look! I am here!"

With a great cry of joy, the princess threw her arms around her sweetheart, as he explained:

"The wicked spell of the Witch Sarabos is all over now, because my friend, the magician, changed me back to normal. He is waiting to take us to see your father, so that we can get married at last. Then, I shall take you back to my kingdom, and we shall be happy for always. Nobody will ever harm you again!"

Hand in hand, the prince and Flora went down the stairs to the magician, who was waiting for them. And no sooner had they entered his coach, than they were at the royal palace.

Seeing them together, the queen flew into the most terrible rage. But the king was so happy to see his daughter that he commanded that the wedding be celebrated without delay.

As for Fish-Face, mad with fury, and green with envy, she was turned into a fish by the magician! And she spent the rest of her days in a fish-pond in the woods.

Gilda and the White Lake

Gilda was a little girl who lived in a small village which was almost hidden by the ice and snow at the foot of a high mountain. When our story begins, the winter had already lasted many months, stroking its frosty fingers all along the bare branches of the trees, and covering all the paths in a thick, white blanket of snow.

Gilda and her friends loved playing in the snow, having snowball fights, or racing their toboggans, the tracks soon vanishing as clouds of snowflakes fell deep and thick.

And how Gilda loved to see the snowflakes dancing in the air, twirling in a soft winter breeze or swirling in a storm. Then they caught on her eyelashes, powdered her nose, her cheeks, and melted on her pink tongue as she caught them on her lips.

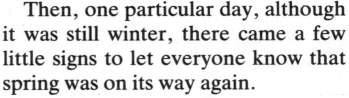

Then, one particular day, although it was still winter, there came a few little signs to let everyone know that spring was on its way again.

Trickles of water began flowing more freely, carrying half-melted slabs of ice with it.

The chirps of birds could be heard as the first rays of the sun appeared, and spring flowers began to poke their heads through the soil.

The children met as usual to decide what to do during the afternoon, Gilda's long, fair hair lifted a little by the breeze as she called for her friend, Natalie.

"Let's begin the last few days of winter with a sleigh ride!" Gilda suggested. "After all, there soon won't be enough snow to do it until next winter!"

"Great!" exclaimed the girls' two brothers, Peter and John. "Good idea, Gilda!"

And off they went to fetch Rudolph, the old reindeer.

"Where shall we go?" asked Natalie, as soon as she was warmly wrapped up in her little blanket. "You know that nightfall comes quickly – and there are still wolves roaming around!"

"Ha! Cowardy-custard!" the boys mocked her. "Why, wolves are only found in fairy stories!"

"Don't worry, Natalie!" added Gilda. "Dear old Rudolph can still run fast enough!" And she stroked the velvety nose of their pet reindeer. "Do you know," she went on, getting into the sleigh, "that in the white lake there is a fish so huge and hungry that it eats all the others! Why, Father Valentine is alway talking about it!"

"Why don't we go and find out, then?" said Peter with a laugh. "Sounds like the one that got away to me!"

And just a few minutes later, the sleigh was gliding silently along the snowy mountain path, with Rudolph knowing exactly which way to go. Peter did not even have to direct him once, he just trotted gently along, his sleigh bells jingling in the soft mountain air.

Rudolph pulled the sleigh through a large forest of fir trees, then they came out on to a gently sloping stretch of land where the grass was already peeping out from beneath the blanket of snow. Here, the waters of the white lake rippled gently along, free of ice, with a boat bobbing up and down.

All the children jumped out of the sledge, then un-harnessed Rudolph so that he could rub his antlers against the tree trunks, as reindeer do.

"Whose is that boat?" Gilda wondered.

"It belongs to the foresters who come here to fish in the spring!" John told her. "They sometimes bring trout for my father to buy!"

"Couldn't we borrow it?" asked Gilda, her eyes sparkling.

"It is too small," Natalie pointed out, wisely staying on the bank. "And it is still cold!"

"Well, it is big enough for me!" retorted Gilda. "You go and have a walk, and let me stay here to fish!"

"Hoping to get Father Valentine's great big fish?" they teased.

But they all knew that once Gilda had made up her mind about something, it was useless to argue with her. So, they left her there and went off for a walk by the stream, with Peter calling out mockingly:

"Don't forget to call us if you need help with the Monster of the Lake!"

"I'm all right by myself!" Gilda shouted back with a laugh.

Very quickly, she untied the boat then jumped aboard like a real sailor and rowed to the middle of the lake. Then she rested the oars, unable to stop herself from leaning over the side. . . but the clear waters of the lake revealed no sign of their mystery. . . the famous fish was nowhere to be seen. . .

"All right, then!" grumbled Gilda. "If I cannot catch Father Valentine's monster fish, I shall try for a few little tiddlers! I'm not going to have the boys laughing at me!"

She found a length of fishing line left in the bottom of the boat by the foresters, then broke off a piece of bread which she hooked on to the line, and lowered it into the water. A long time passed without anything happening at all. Then, the line jerked. . . Gilda pulled. . . and a tiny little fish dangled at the end!

"How sad you look!" cried Gilda, seeing the desperate efforts of the little creature to free itself, flapping the air with its fins. "Why, I'm afraid to even touch you for fear of tearing your little mouth! But, do not worry – I shall put you in the water, and you can soon free yourself!"

No sooner said than done! Gilda lowered the line and the fish back down into the lake.

And that was the start of a very strange adventure, because only about five minutes later, the line jerked again.

Gilda pulled away happily – and found another fish at the end, just a little bigger than her hand. She looked at it doubtfully.

"What are you doing here?" she demanded. "I don't need you! I want a fish lots bigger for my friends and myself!"

So, once again, she threw back her catch.

Somehow, the lake seemed to understand just what Gilda wanted, and how much catching a good-sized fish meant to her, because the line tugged again soon afterwards – and there was a fairly large fish at the end of it!

Gilda was delighted. But, just as she unhooked it, the fish escaped at once into the water with a swish of its tail!

Then the line unravelled itself very quickly – so quickly, in fact, that the whole skein seemed to tumble through Gilda's hands, almost completely disappearing into the water before her very eyes.

Gilda was so disappointed, she almost cried. Such a fine fish, and it had gone! The two boys would never believe that she had got such a fine catch!

All she could do now was to sit there holding on to the line and keep hoping. . .

But with nothing much else to do, everything seemed so boring with time so long and completely endless – so much for the pleasures of fishing, Gilda thought. Sitting in the middle of the white lake, Gilda began to wish that she had gone with her friends.

Suddenly, there was another tug at the line. Gilda tightened her grip, ready to pull it in a little. Again the line pulled, then slackened, giving Gilda chance to grip rather more tightly. This went on until almost the whole length of line was back in the lake. Gilda just could not understand it.

All at once, the line began to quiver between her fingers. She tried with all her might to hold it – but it seemed to shake itself from one side to the other, making the boat rock dangerously. Gilda just managed to wind the end of the line on to the stern of the boat, and then she looked into the waters of the lake. . .

It was then that she saw a fish so enormous that she could hardly believe her own eyes! Her heart beating fast, she made sure that the line was fastened tightly before beginning to row slowly and carefully towards the bank, silently praying that the enormous fish would not struggle too much and make the boat capsize. . .

But, as she rowed into shallower waters, the great big fish beat its tail more and more strongly, tiring Gilda out as she put all her strength behind the oars, trying to row to the side of the lake. Taking a deep breath, she began crying out with all her might.

"Natalie! Peter! John! Come quickly and help me!"

Gilda knew that every second counted, before the fish had time to get its strength back!

The two boys ran up first, and with scornful giggles, called out:

"Come on, Gilda! Show us the whale you've caught!"

"Idiots!" yelled Gilda, pulling frantically on the oars. "Come and help me – quickly, before it escapes!"

That was when the boys, much to their amazement, saw the enormous fish flapping about in the shallow water. They ran towards the bank, and John jumped on board to help Gilda pull on the line, whilst Peter hauled the boat on to dry land. Natalie came running a good way behind, but she caught hold of the end of the line and held it firmly.

With one last burst of desperation and energy, the huge fish lashed out with great sweeps of its tail and its fins.

Little by little, the children drew near to the edge of the lake, and lifted the enormous fish between them, with much puffing and panting, and lots of shouts and cheers.

Then, inch by inch, they managed to drag it on to the bank.

The fish was all in by this time. The children cheered each other once again, with Natalie, Peter and John all hugging Gilda with glee.

Then Gilda took the fish by the tail, John took the head, and between them they carried it up to the mountain path. Rudolph, his brown eyes wide in amazement, started a little at seeing such a strange load. Never in his whole reindeer life had he seen such an enormous fish!

But they had to hurry now, because they had to return home by nightfall and already the sun was setting.

The two brothers managed to haul the fish on to the sleigh, whilst the girls made themselves comfortable, Natalie sharing her seat with Gilda's wonderful catch!

Rudolph trotted along happily, looking forward to being back in his stable – after being the centre of attraction, pulling his unforgettable load through the village!

Of course, Gilda's friends wanted to know exactly what had happened, so she was soon telling them all about her adventure – much to the sorrow and envy of the two boys, who now bitterly regretted that they had not stayed with her. Still, they were happy enough to come home with such a splendid catch.

"Father Valentine will be so jealous!" said John. "He's been trying for months to get this fish! How disappointed he's going to be when he hears how you have succeeded where he has failed, Gilda!"

"And wait till he finds out that is is a girl who has taken the prize from under his nose!" grinned Natalie.

"But, I am not a complete beginner!" Gilda protested, tossing back her long, fair hair. "I have been on fishing trips with my daddy, almost since I was a baby, even catching trout in my hand from the stream! Those trout are very cunning, too, but I know where to catch them!"

Natalie looked at her friend with much admiration, thinking how brave Gilda was. . . when a low cry sounded near at hand, followed by a low, mournful-sounding howl. . .

121

There was no mistaking that sound. Wolves were about!

The children looked anxiously at each other, and all the bedtime stories they had heard began to flood into their minds.

"Faster, Rudolph!" urged John. "Faster!" But Rudolph was already running at the sound of those first howls.

As it happened, they were right in the centre of the forest, when, jaws open and dark eyes gleaming, the wild beasts came out from between the trees.

"Faster, Rudolph!" shouted John again, shaking the reins.

But, oh dear! Rudolph was going as fast as his old hooves could carry him – and the wolves were still gaining ground.

Then, from a dark sky, snowflakes began to fall, making the whole forest black and menacing. Pale and frightened, the children thought no more of their splendid catch of fish. . .

Now, they could almost feel the hot breath of the wolves on their necks!

"We must do something!" Gilda kept saying, nibbling at her glove in fear. "We must do something, quickly – but, what?"

Then, almost without thinking, she took hold of the enormous fish by its gills, and, threw it behind the sleigh with all her strength, right under the wolves' noses.

And a very strange thing happened. The enormous fish was still on the end of the line – so, as Gilda threw it, a second, smaller fish sprang out of the mouth of the big one, and began to fly along behind the sleigh, bumping over the powdery snow. . .

Meanwhile, the hungry wolves fell upon the enormous fish with relish, giving the children time to make a good getaway. And it was not a second too soon, because, all at once, a whole pack appeared!

"Faster! Faster, my good, brave Rudolph!" cried John, spurring on the old reindeer just as much as he possibly could.

But, it was all in vain, Rudolph could do no more – because, just then, they were faced with still more trouble. . . The runners of the sleigh began sinking deeply down into the soft snow, and soon they were going slower than ever!

Suddenly, Gilda had an idea, and went to sit at the back of the sleigh, the fishing line clenched in her hand. . .

When the first wolves began to overtake the sleigh, they turned round as they saw a golden, appetising-looking fish right under their noses. With one bound, they all went behind as Gilda carried on tugging at the line. Then, when she could see that they were all getting tired with the chase, she flung the fish from the line as far as she could, with the wolves, still ever eager for food, racing after it. Only one, very little fish remained now. . .

All the children breathed sighs of relief as the sleigh began to gather speed once more.

And, as the forest began to clear and the sky lightened a little, they

all began hoping again, especially when Rudolph was able to go at a trot along the straight path at the edge of the forest.

Thoughtfully, Gilda considered the tiny fish she had caught first of all, now bouncing along on the end of the line behind the sleigh.

"It can hardly be seen. . ." she admitted. "But, perhaps it will do for the one, hungry wolf which is left. . ."

And, luckily, Gilda was right. That one wolf, seeing that the sleigh was approaching the edge of the forest where wild animals did not dare to go, he decided to settle for that last, smallest fish of all.

With just one bite, he had gobbled up the smallest catch of all. Then, with tail down and tongue hanging out, he went back into the depth of the forest, giving one last, long howl, to which the rest of the pack replied, already beginning to hunt after bigger prey. . .

127

Rudolph was very tired by this time, but somehow he gathered his strength, and very soon the sledge was speeding down towards the village, with the children snuggled comfortably together.

Never had they been so pleased to see their village crouched so cosily at the foot of the high mountain! At the sight of the first chimneys, they burst into song, so glad to smell the burning wood fires with the promise of hot soup, a warm welcome and a safe end to their journey.

Caught by the mountain and bathed in pink and violet, the sun was going to bed as Rudolph neared the first row of houses, with windows lit from all sides as they passed. The little village square was empty, because it was now supper-time. Only the children's parents waited anxiously. . . None of the boys or girls had ever been out so late.

And when, at long last, they heard Rudolph's bells, they ran out in front of the sledge, laughing and crying all at once with welcome and relief to see their children safe and sound.

So happy were they, that the grown-ups did not have the heart to scold the foolish children, especially when they heard about the danger they had been in, because of the wolves.

Hugging the children very close, all the parents shivered without stopping, remembering all the children from the same village who had disappeared in the forest over the years. In the end, they promised themselves that they would have a big hunt in order to get rid of those wolves, once and for all.

But now was the time for joy and celebration! Very soon, there was quite a crowd at Gilda's home – nobody even thought about finishing supper! They all wanted to hear about her adventure!

So, once the children were seated comfortably by the fire to get warm, and given big mugs of lovely, hot drinking chocolate, Gilda began to tell the story of the marvellous fish.

But it seemed she was forever being interrupted by people wanting to know more!

"Really?"

"The fish was so very large, Gilda?"

"Yes!" nodded Peter and John at once. "We saw it!"

With Peter and John backing her up, everyone could see that Gilda was telling the truth. Natalie also added a few details here and there, but she was still rather dazed by all that had happened.

As for the older people, they did not even think of making fun of Gilda when she opened her arms wide to show how big the fish had been.

"Didn't I tell you, so many times?" groaned Father Valentine.

Then the boys explained how the wolves had descended upon the huge fish thrown by clever Gilda. And, as she paused to draw breath, the two brothers went on to tell everyone about the end of the chase, and how brave poor old Rudolph had been as he struggled in the snow, when the sleigh runners had got stuck.

And how everyone clapped and cheered when Gilda reported how she had thrown the second little fish under the jaws of the wildest wolf, so that they could escape into the safer part of the forest!

"My word!" shouted Father Valentine. "Our Fishing Club will have to make you a Member of Honour after this!"

"Good idea!" cried the villagers. "We shall give you a medal for being so brave and so clever, Gilda!"

And so it was that the story of Gilda and The White Lake became quite a legend in and around that little mountain village. Naughty children often heard about her, as an example of what could happen to those who were a little too daring. After all – what would have happened in that thick, dark forest if the children had had no fish to throw to those wolves?

The Four Little Girls

Mrs. Flowers was a lady whose husband had been killed in the wars, and she lived happily enough with her two little girls, Carolyn and Melanie, in a big house with a pretty garden all around it.

Eight-year-old Carolyn had a gay and lively nature, whilst Melanie, just one year younger, was rather more quiet.

One summer's day, Carolyn, Melanie and their maid, Eleanor went for a walk in the country, not too far from home, to pick some wild flowers.

But on the way, they suddenly saw a carriage where the horses were rearing up with all their might, pulling it this way and that. And inside there was a young woman and a little girl, crying out in fear.

As Carolyn, Melanie and Eleanor hurried forward, the coach and the horses gave a sudden lurch into the ditch with an ear-splitting crash.

The two little girls and their maid at once ran up to see if the two passengers or their coachman needed help. Luckily, the man and the little girl were not seriously hurt. But the young woman was quite badly injured, and so the coachman, Eleanor and the children helped her as quickly as possible to the Flowers' home.

During the short journey, Carolyn and Melanie tried to comfort the little girl, who was so upset to see that her mother had been hurt.

Mrs. Flowers also felt very sorry for the girl and her mother, and offered to put up both the lady, Mrs. Rose, and her daughter Greta, who had just had her fourth birthday.

And, during the days which followed, she looked after both the mother and daughter with great care.

When Mrs. Rose was well enough, she told them that she had been without any news of her husband for three years. He had been the captain of a steamship which she now believed had been sunk at sea. After having had so much sadness, it was a great comfort to her to have the friendship of Mrs. Flowers.

"Why should we be separated, my dear? This home and our hearts are big enough to have you here for always! I should be so happy if you could look upon me as a sister, and your dear Greta would be just as happy with my Carolyn and Melanie! I beg you, please accept my offer and allow me a very great pleasure. We have both been very lonely women for far too long!"

"With a thousand thanks, I accept your kind offer!" cried Mrs. Rose. "Come, let us go quickly and give the girls our good news!"

And all the girls were highly delighted. "Marvellous!" they cried together, throwing themselves into their mothers' arms.

And, just to show how pleased they felt, Carolyn, Melanie and Greta began dancing all around the garden, laughing and singing until they had to stop for breath.

Now, not very far from the Flowers, there lived a little girl called Sophie – and she was not very happy. Her father had been ill for many years, but, before he died, he had married a second wife, a lady called Mrs. Pincher, who hated Sophie.

She was always telling people about the naughty things which

Sophie did, and it seemed that the little girl was always doing something to annoy and upset Mrs. Pincher.

Carolyn and Melanie felt sorry for Sophie, and often invited her to come and play at their home.

One day, when the two sisters were busy doing their lessons, Sophie and Greta had gone for a walk to the farmyard, and, on the way they came across a little pond.

Sophie at once had one of her naughty ideas. Climbing up on a stile, she said to her friend:

"Just look at those lovely flowers, Greta! I wonder if we can go and pick them?"

"No, Sophie," Greta told her. "It's not allowed!"

Sophie shrugged her shoulders, and went up to the edge of the pond, bending down and holding out her hand. Suddenly, she let out a scream and vanished into the water.

"Hold on!" shouted Greta, trying to reach Sophie. But she did not have enough strength to reach her friend. . . Instead, she fell into the green waters of the pond, herself!

Luckily for them, the men from the farm had heard Greta's cries. They ran up with their rods and their rakes and managed to reach the two girls. Very soon, they had been brought to Mrs. Flowers' home, where everyone there began comforting them as they rubbed them dry with warm towels.

But, oh dear! It was at that very moment that the cruel Mrs. Pincher decided to arrive. And when she saw Sophie, wet and covered with mud, she went pale with anger and shook the poor little girl very hard indeed.

"What have I told you?" she screamed. "You have dared ruin your new clothes by not looking where you were going and falling into the pond? You wait! I shall punish you, just as you deserve!"

And before anyone could stop her, the woman took a heavy candlestick from her bag and rushed at Sophie, lashing out at her in anger, and shouting that she would be locked up for eight days in the cellar, alone and in darkness, and with nothing to eat except dry bread and water. All the time she was hitting poor Sophie with the candlestick until it broke between her fingers, then she threw down the pieces, red-faced with fury, and went to leave the room. Mrs. Flowers hurried after her, trying to sooth Mrs. Pincher's temper. But she would not listen.

"Believe me," Mrs. Pincher insisted, "there is just one way of bringing up a child correctly. To my mind, the whip is the best of teachers! I know of none better, especially with a child as bold and as naughty as Sophie!"

So all Mrs. Flowers could do was to show the dreadful woman out of her house as quickly as possible. But she felt so sorry for poor little Sophie. Sophie was sometimes naughty, she agreed, but that was no reason to deprive her of care and kindness. Yet she knew it was no good talking to hard-hearted Mrs. Pincher.

So when Mrs. Rose and Greta came back, they were amazed to find Carolyn and Melanie in floods of tears, and to see Sophie in her petticoat sobbing so miserably, with bruises all over her body as a result of the beating by her step-mother.

All through the evening, they did their best to help Sophie cheer up, even making up their minds to be friends with Mrs. Pincher.

A few weeks later, Carolyn received a letter from Sophie, asking her to come to lunch along with Melanie, Mrs. Flowers, Greta and Mrs. Rose. With just a little smile at all Sophie's spelling mistakes, Carolyn put the letter in her pocket, and went to tell Mrs. Flowers about Mrs. Pincher's invitation.

"Mummy!" she called out. "Sophie has written to say that Mrs. Pincher asks us to come to lunch tomorrow afternoon!"

"Oh, yes?" replied Mrs. Flowers, very slowly. "So, what's going on? Would you like to go, Carolyn?"

Carolyn thought how happy Sophie would be to see them all again, so she answered:

"Yes, I would, Mummy. I like Sophie very much, and I feel sorry for her, being so ill-treated!"

"Yes, she has been scolded and punished too often for my liking," agreed Mrs. Flowers. "Mind you, she's always getting into mischief. . ."

"But, Mummy!" Carolyn burst out. "Surely she has paid for all that by now!

Mrs. Flowers couldn't help agreeing with Carolyn, and she nodded her head thoughtfully.

"Yes, Carolyn," she sighed, "that is certainly true. . . Very well, you may tell her that we shall come tomorrow."

Carolyn thanked her mother, then she went to ask Melanie and Greta to sign their names on the note to send back to Sophie.

And next day, they all went together to Mrs. Pincher's house. Before long, she was saying how much she wanted to be rid of Sophie, because she wanted to go on a long holiday. Mrs. Flowers, thinking that Sophie would soon mend her ways, being with the other three little girls, at once offered to take Sophie home with her – and Mrs. Pincher was so pleased!

The four little girls were simply delighted to be together again at Mrs. Flowers' house. But, far from becoming good and well-behaved like her friends, Sophie was still very naughty and silly.

It was soon discovered that Sophie was also dreadfully greedy. One day, when Mrs. Flowers had sent the girls to pick redcurrants to make jam, Sophie ate such a lot instead, that she became quite ill and had to stay in bed for three whole days.

Another day, Sophie happened to be talking to Greta when she worked herself up into such a rage that she hit Greta round the ear – and that meant she had to be punished by staying alone in her room without any tea, whilst the others were out in the sunshine, playing games and having fun.

Oh, dear! It seemed so hard for naughty little Sophie to learn to be good! Each time she got into any kind of trouble, she would try hard to be good and not to lose her temper again. . . but, sooner or later, she would find herself slippng back into her old ways, and getting into some kind of mischief.

One day, Mrs. Flowers and Melanie had gone into the village, leaving Mrs. Rose in the living room with Carolyn.

Sophie was playing alone in the garden, thinking of Carolyn and Melanie, and how they always tried to help everyone they met. She began wishing that she could be the same.

At last, she went to find Greta, and asked her:

"Greta, would you help me with this idea I have? I'd love to take out all the savings in my money-box to give to that poor old lady who lives on the other side of the woods!"

"I don't mind, if mummy says that we can," said Greta, not bothering to look up from dressing her doll. "Why don't we go and ask her?"

"Oh, but there's no need to ask her, is there?" pleaded Sophie. "Let's keep it all a nice secret!"

And Sophie seemed to want to be good and kind so much, that Greta agreed.

So the two girls went to get the money, and then began walking deep into the woods.

But night-fall came all too quickly, before they had even come across another village or single house.

"I am so tired. . ." cried Greta, beginning to weep bitter tears. "And I am so hungry. . . I-I do not like the dark, either. . ."

Sophie did not feel very brave herself by this time.

"Oh, Greta. . ." she wailed. "I-I am so sorry! I don't know the way – and, th-that means we are lost!"

And with these words, she burst into tears as well.

Shivering with cold and sobbing with fright, the two little girls began to walk into the unknown, with pines, nettles and brambles seeming to lash out at them, and clawing at their legs and arms.

Then suddenly, they heard the sound of twigs cracking, strange, fierce-sounding growls, then steps coming nearer. . . And when Greta felt a blast of hot breath on the back of her neck, she let out such a scream.

Sophie gripped her hand, and together they began to run in wild desperation. By chance, they came across some low tree branches, and tried to climb up higher in the hope of escape. . .

At that very moment, a beam of moonlight crossed the clouds, and they saw a big, wild boar which was pacing around down below. They had just managed to escape the most terrible danger!

Sophie and Greta were both trembling so much that their teeth chattered. And, at last, when the wild boar turned away, they heard the distant sound of a cart coming through the woods.

"Help!" they cried. "Help!"

The woodcutter who was driving the cart was soon able to find the two little girls, and took them at once back to Mrs. Flowers, where everyone was almost frantic with worry.

And when all the excitement was over, Sophie made up her mind to try and become as sensible as her friends. But, this time, she really meant it.

During the days which followed the dangerous escapade in the woods, Carolyn complained of having headaches and feeling very hot and shivery. Her face looked so thin and so pale that Mrs. Flowers was very worried, and she called in the doctor.

He said it was chicken-pox, and said that the other three children should be sent away so that they would not be ill, too.

So Mrs. Flowers and Eleanor stayed behind with Carolyn, and looked after her. But – how slowly the time went by for Melanie, Greta and Sophie, without Carolyn to make them laugh and sing. They tried to while away the hours with sewing and knitting.

Meanwhile, Carolyn was getting better, well enough to potter around the house, once Eleanor said that she need not stay in bed all the time. But, after nursing Carolyn for so long, she began to feel unwell herself, and was soon very ill.

"It's all my fault that Eleanor is ill!" cried Carolyn, very upset. "So it is up to me to look after her!"

And all the time that Eleanor was unwell, Carolyn helped Mrs. Flowers to look after her, doing all she could to make Eleanor feel better.

At last, the doctor came and said that both Carolyn and Eleanor were quite well enough to see their friends once again!

Mad with delight at the idea of leaving their sick-room and breathing fresh air, Carolyn clattered down the stairs to go and re-join her friends and her sister.

"Melanie!" she cried out. "Greta! Sophie! Eleanor and I are better now!"

And how happy they all were to be together again after being apart for so long! There was so much to tell each other!

And, as the doctor had also said that Eleanor and Carolyn should go out into the fresh air and get the colour back in their cheeks, it was the perfect excuse to explore the big garden once again, and see all the new flowers poking up, to herald the spring-time.

"My dear girls," Mrs. Flowers said one day, "I think we shall go for a nice, long walk. The weather is lovely, so we shall go into the woods, up near the old windmill!"

Pleased at the idea of such a treat, the girls went to ask Eleanor to prepare a basket of food, then they brushed their straw hats.

The walk was lovely, then everyone sat down in the shade of some old oak trees. And, as the girls picked some wild berries, they thought they heard a slight noise. . . So they stopped and listened – and sure enough, the sound of sobs and tears came to their ears.

All four of them turned in the direction of the noise – and, very soon, they saw a poor little girl of about twelve, dressed in rags and crying as though her heart would break. They all went up to her to see if there was anything they could do to help.

"What is the matter?" asked Melanie, offering the girl her handkerchief.

"I-I am crying," sobbed the girl, "because my mother is ill! We have no money to buy food, and as we have only just come to live in these parts, we know absolutely nobody who we can ask for help!"

Greta felt so sorry for the girl. So, very firmly, she took hold of her hand.

"Look, you stay here!" she said. "We shall bring my mother, and she will know what to do!"

Before very long, Mrs. Rose had arrived, and she asked the little girl what her mother's name was. The girl answered without lifting her eyes from the ground.

"My mother's name is Frigate, but only because she is a sailor's wife. But my father. . . he has been lost at sea for many years, now. . ."

By this time, Mrs. Rose was looking very upset, as though she was about to start crying herself.

"On which ship did your father sail, my dear?" she asked gently, her voice trembling a little. "Who was the captain?"

"It - it was the Frigate Sybil," faltered the little girl, "under the command of Captain Rose!"

Mrs. Rose gave a little cry, and, taking the girl's hand, asked if she would take her to see her mother.

The girl was named Lucy, and she took them all to a lonely cabin, where she lived with her mother. Mrs. Rose introduced herself, and said to the poor woman:

"I have wept, just like you, for my lost husband. His ship has sunk, there can be no doubt, otherwise we would have had news a long, long time ago. But – who knows if our poor husbands are not ship-wrecked somewhere far away, waiting to come back to us, some day? We must not give up hope, my dear! Please wait with me for better days to come, I beg you!"

And so it was that Mrs. Frigate and her daughter Lucy left their cabin to come and live near the Flowers' house in a dear little cottage which Mrs. Rose had built for her.

What was more, the little girls had yet another nice friend!

And after she had lived with the Flowers for over a year, Sophie had become so happy, knowing that she was with a family who truly loved her and cared about her. She had almost forgotten her step-mother – until, one morning, Mrs. Flowers told her:

"Sophie, dear – your step-mother has written a letter. . ."

Without even giving Mrs. Flowers the chance to finish talking, poor Sophie began trembling. She threw herself into the woman's arms and began to cry.

She was so upset, but Mrs. Flowers stroked her hair comfortingly.

"Look dear," she said comfortingly, "if you think that your step-mother is coming to take you away, let me tell you that she has said that she wants you to stay here, with us. She has gone abroad and married a rich count who does not want any children around. She has asked me to find a Boarding School for you. . ."

Sophie looked at Mrs. Flowers with such a sad face that she hurried on with a smile:

"That is, your step-mother adds, if I do not want to keep you here, you young rascal! So, what do you think, dear? You must decide what you really want to do!"

"Oh, dear, dear Mrs. Flowers," cried Sophie, "please keep me here for ever, with you. You are my real family, now!"

Mrs. Flowers took Sophie in her arms and gave her a hug.

"Then that is settled, Sophie. You can be my little girl, the same as Carolyn and Melanie. I know that you would much rather

be with us than at the finest school in the country!"

Sophie threw her arms around Mrs. Flowers' waist and held her close.

"Dear Mrs. Flowers... thank you, so much! Of course, I-I do know that I shall cost quite a lot of money for you to keep me here..."

Mrs. Flowers chuckled.

"Do not worry about that!" she told Sophie. "Your father left some money for you, and that will be more than enough for everything you need!"

Sophie hugged Mrs. Flowers yet again, then she rushed out to give the marvellous news to all her friends. And, what joy there was! They danced around so wildly that Eleanor had to leave her cooking to go and see what all the noise was about.

"What on earth is happening?" she exclaimed. "What's all this fuss about?"

So Greta pulled Eleanor into the room, and began to explain all over again.

"Sophie is ours for always, Eleanor! Mrs. Pincher has married again! She's the wife of Count Louis Blagowski, and they don't want Sophie living with them! Isn't that wonderful?"

Eleanor was just as delighted as everyone else.

"We shall have to give a party!" she announced. "A proper celebration, with fairy lights in all the trees!"

Overjoyed at having such a treat, the girls all sat down to make paper roses, lanterns and party garlands!

Eleanor, who was a splendid cook, made a big plum tart with chocolate creams, cake and lots of other good things.

Next day, the weather was warm and sunny. And after lunch, Carolyn, Melanie, Greta, Lucy and Sophie took the donkeys for a lovely long ride into the woods, with Eleanor and the three mothers following behind.

Once they arrived at a clearing, the children stopped.

And, whilst the donkeys rested, the children, Mrs. Rose, Mrs. Flowers and Mrs. Frigate and Eleanor played Hide-and-Seek and I-Spy – and then, how they enjoyed all Eleanor's goodies!

All too soon, evening came, so everyone had to go back to the Flowers' home, where Lucy's mother lit the fairy lights which shone like a million stars on the balcony.

"Th-thank you," cried Sophie, sobbing with happiness, "thank you, my dear friends. . ."